VALLEY VIEW
HEALTH CENTER
OUR
LITERACY
COUNCIL
Enjoy this book provided by
Twin Cities Rotary Club,
Valley View Health Center,
and Our Literacy Council.
W9-CKG-910
DISCARD

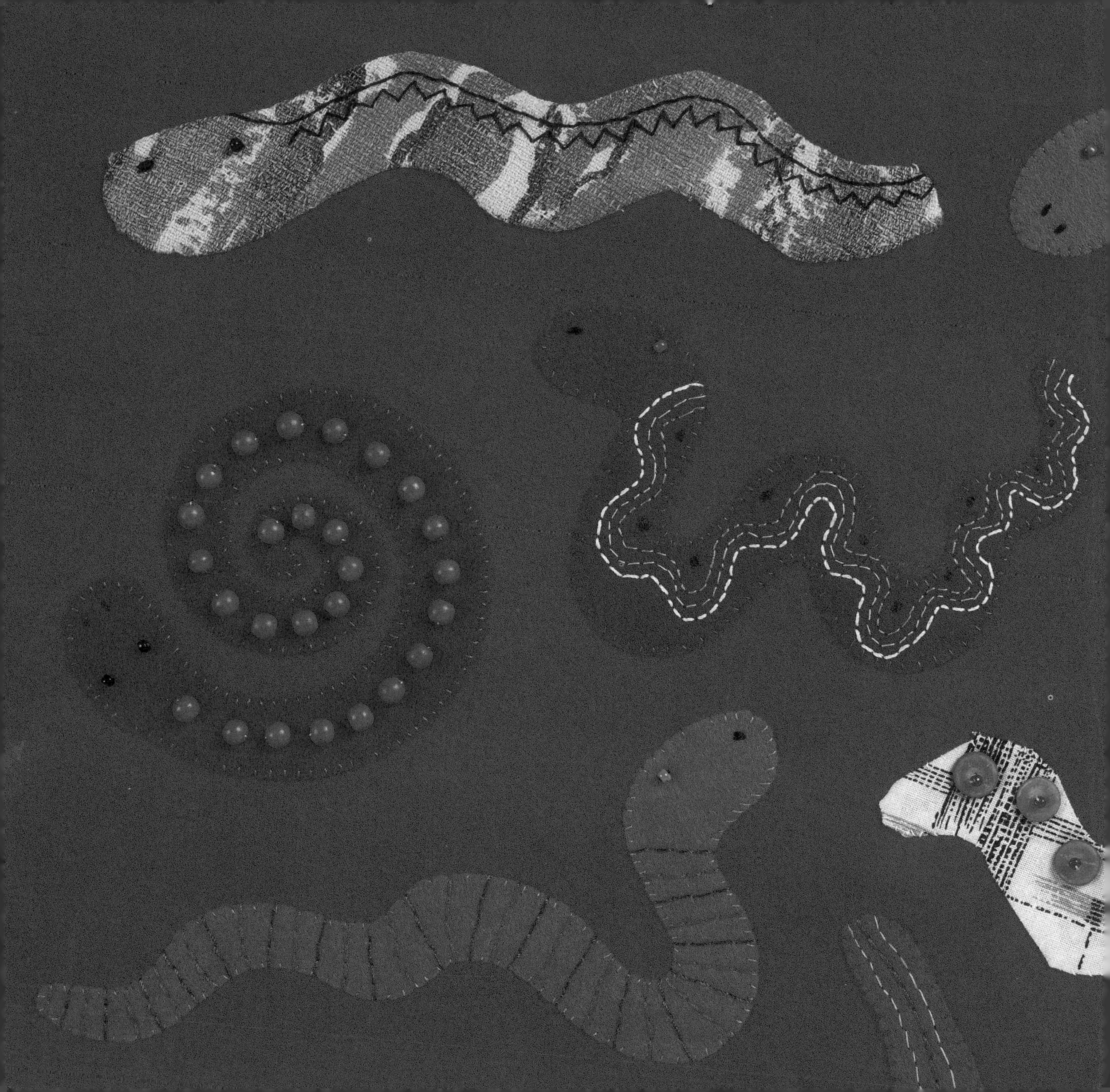

HOW LOUD IS A LION?

Clare Beaton

Barefoot Books
Celebrating Art and Story

Parrots are feathery, porcupines are prickly,
But how loud is a lion? Shhh! Listen!

Giraffes are gentle, gazelles are graceful,
But how loud is a lion? Shhh! Listen!

Cheetahs are spotty, zebras are stripy,
But how loud is a lion? Shhh! Listen!

Hoopoes are happy, chimpanzees are sneaky,
But how loud is a lion? Shhh! Listen!

Chameleons are colorful, snakes are slithery,
But how loud is a lion? Shhh! Listen!

**Antelopes are elegant, elephants are enormous,
But how loud is a lion? Shhh! Listen!**

Crocodiles are crafty, monkeys are mischievous,
But how loud is a lion? Shhh! Listen!

Gorillas are grizzly, zorillas are greedy,
But how loud is a lion? Shhh! Listen!

Hippos are heavy, rhinos are hefty,
But how loud is a lion? Shhh! Listen!

ROA

RR!!!

Shhh!

Praise for Clare Beaton

There's a Cow in the Cabbage Patch
"The magical blend of flannel boards and quilting is like eye candy — a visual feast for the mind and the soul" — *Booklist*

How Big is a Pig?
"Bold, bright tableaux...a sassy, unexpected wrap-up; Beaton will have her audience's attention all sewn up" — *Publishers Weekly*

One Moose, Twenty Mice
"Young viewers will find the fuzzy menagerie endearing, and they'll giggle through the rollicking kitty hunt" — *Bulletin of the Center for Children's Books*

Zoë and her Zebra
"A visually tactile phantasmagoria...the illustrations beg to be touched" — *School Library Journal*

For my daughter, Kate – C. B.
For Francis – S. B.

Barefoot Books
3 Bow Street, 3rd Floor
Cambridge, MA 02138

First published in the United States of America in 2002 by Barefoot Books, Inc.

This book was typeset in Plantin Schoolbook Bold 20 on 28 point
The illustrations were prepared in felt with braid, beads and sequins
Graphic design by Judy Linard, London. Color transparencies by Jonathan Fisher Photography, Bath
Color separation by Grafiscan, Italy. Printed and bound in Singapore by Tien Wah Press Pte Ltd
This book has been printed on 100% acid-free paper

Hardback ISBN 1-84148-896-8

1 3 5 7 9 8 6 4 2

U.S. Cataloging-in-Publication Data (Library of Congress Standards)

Blackstone, Stella.
How loud is a lion? / [Stella Blackstone] ; Clare Beaton. 1st ed.
[24] p. : col. ill. ; cm.
Note: "The moral right of Stella Blackstone to be identified as the author and Clare Beaton to be identified as the illustrator of this work has been asserted" [last page of text]
Summary: Different animals of the jungle are presented through descriptive adjectives and repeating text.
ISBN 1 84148-896-8
1. Lions — Fiction. 2. Wild animals — Fiction. 3. Stories in rhyme. I. Beaton, Clare. II. Title.
[E] 21 2002 AC CIP

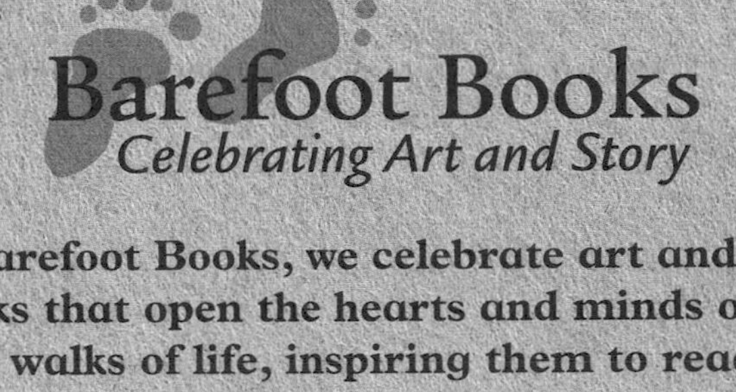

At Barefoot Books, we celebrate art and story with books that open the hearts and minds of children from all walks of life, inspiring them to read deeper, search further, and explore their own creative gifts. Taking our inspiration from many different cultures, we focus on themes that encourage independence of spirit, enthusiasm for learning, and acceptance of other traditions. Thoughtfully prepared by writers, artists and storytellers from all over the world, our products combine the best of the present with the best of the past to educate our children as the caretakers of tomorrow.

www.barefootbooks.com

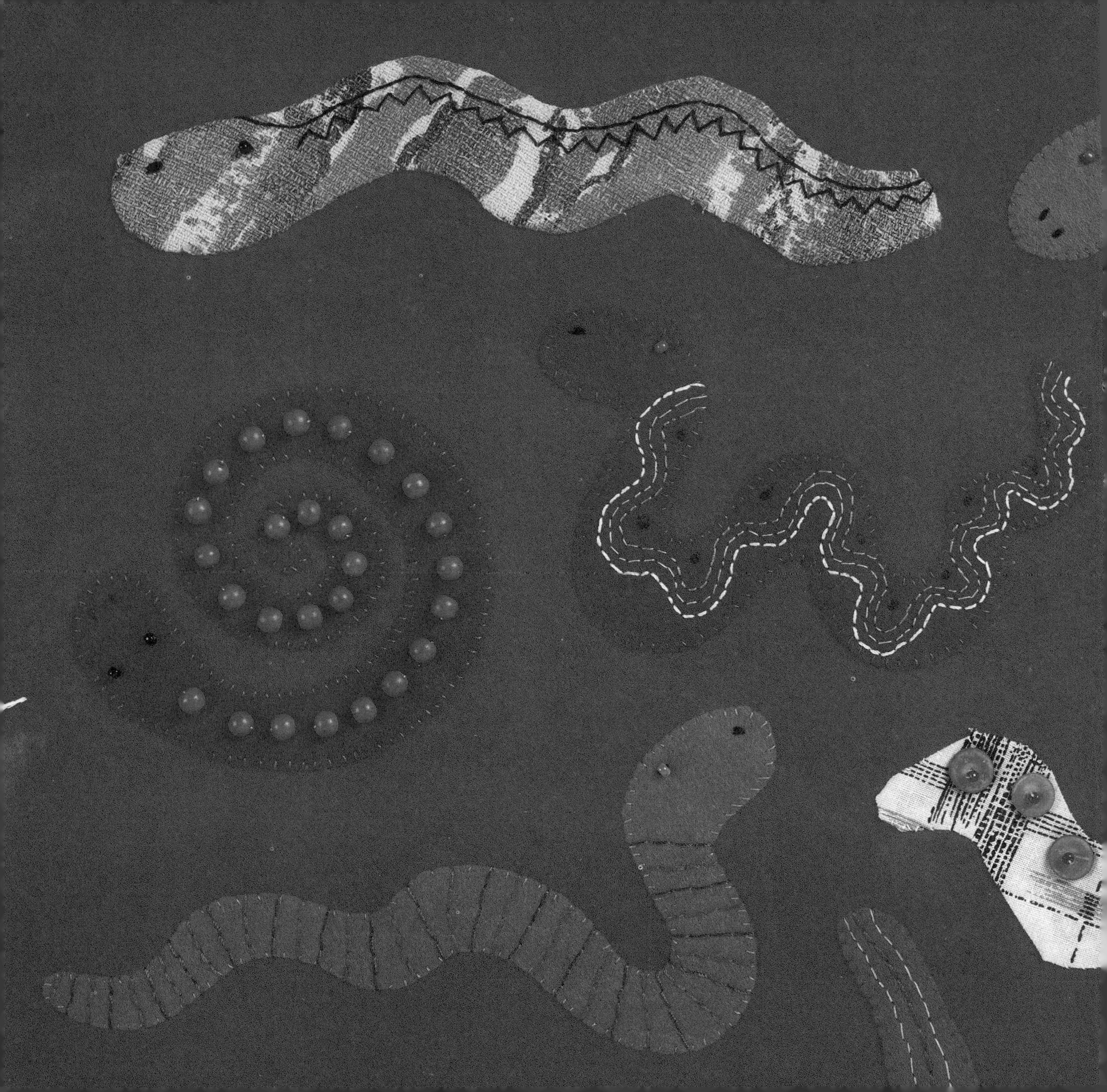